W9-AUT-420

Good Babies, Bad Babies

Good Babies
Bad Babies

JOHN LAWRENCE

David R. Godine, *Publisher*
BOSTON

First U.S. edition published in 1990 by
DAVID R. GODINE, PUBLISHER
Horticultural Hall
300 Massachusetts Avenue
Boston, Massachusetts 02115

ISBN 0-87923-823-2
LC 89-46200

First U.S. edition
Printed in Hong Kong

FOR TRISTAN

Good Babies

Bad Babies

sweet ones, sour ones

bald ones, curly ones

big ones

small ones

and sometimes . . .

old fashioned ones

black ones

white ones

fat ones

fin ones

and also very . . .

clever ones

loud ones

soft ones

high ones

low ones

and even . . .

dreams of glory ones

polite ones

rude ones

bouncing ones

tired ones

and lastly . . .

bye bye baby ones